I WILL HOLD
MY DEATH CLOSE

THE ZOMBIE BIBLE – BOOK 5

STANT LITORE

Westmarch Publishing

2016

– THE SILVER EDITION –

FIRST PUBLISHED IN 2014

The characters and events portrayed in this book are fictitious.
Any similarity to real persons, living or dead, is coincidental and
not intended by the author.

Stant Litore is a pen name for Daniel Fusch.

Cover art © 2016 by Lauren K. Cannon.
Cover design by Roberto Calas.

A Westmarch Publishing release.

ISBN: 978-1-942458-17-3

Previous editions published by 47North, an imprint of Amazon
Publishing.

You can reach Stant Litore at:
http://stantlitore.com
zombiebible@gmail.com
http://www.facebook.com/stant.litore
@thezombiebible

PRAISE FOR STANT LITORE'S
THE ZOMBIE BIBLE

"Heartbreaking and wonderful." – *Conflictium*

"I find myself riveted to Stant's prose, not only because I'm eager to find out the characters' fate but because his words are so beautiful. The story has stayed with me days after reading it. I highly recommend." – Denise Grover Swank, author of *The Curse Keepers*

"Stant Litore has been doing fascinating phantasmagorical things with zombies in biblical times." – Jeff Vandermeer, author of *Annihilation*

"Beautifully composed and frighteningly well-researched… Well worth the read… Beyond the rich historical background and the desperate fight for survival, *Strangers in the Land* is a story about otherness, what it means to be a 'stranger'… Far from being 'just another zombie book', it is a remarkably clear look at what it means to impose a system of inequality among a culture."
– *Examiner.com*

"To say I loved this book would be an understatement. I could not put it down." – *The Seattle Post-Intelligencer*

"*The Zombie Bible* is philosophy played out in bleak landscapes. It's psychology set to the harsh strains of Prokofiev. Litore's prose is lean and hungry; his characters are faceted all-round like various colored stones; his scenes pulse with blood and life, ring with metal or reek of sweat and undeath." – Marc McDermott

"Like Cormac McCarthy's novels, *I Will Hold My Death Close* does not pull its punches. A beautiful, brilliant tale, it offers a pretty bleak picture of the human condition and the human struggle against the terrors of this world." – Andrew Hallam, Ph.D., Metropolitan State University of Denver

"Litore's vibrant writing . . . rips the lid off of the King James version and reveals to us a world of intense human hopes, dreams and pathos, with a liberal dose of horror seething in the shadows. You've never seen anything like this before." – Richard Ellis Preston, Jr., author of *Romulus Buckle and the City of the Founders*

"Intensely troubling and sharply beautiful. I highly anticipate the opportunity to reread it." – Timothy Widman, *Wandering Paths*

"Gruesome and human and lyrical and horrible, *The Zombie Bible* is like nothing you have ever read. Once you're in, you'll stay." – S.G. Redling, author of *Flowertown* and *Damocles*

"Stant rebuilds the zombie mythology from the ground up." – Rob Kroese, author of *Mercury Falls* and *Schrodinger's Gat*

"What Litore has done ... I call it the de-sanitisation of the gospel: a visceral, messy, human take on a message of a visceral and tangible hope." – Siku, creator of *The Manga Bible* and *Drink It!*

"A good novel should go for the throat; *Death Has Come up into Our Windows* goes for your heart, rips it out and eats it before your eyes." – Lucinda Rose, *Rose Reads*

CONTENTS

BASED LOOSELY ON
THE EVENTS OF JUDGES 11

CIRCA 1120 BC

*for the millions of young women
whose names no one remembers*

1

I HAVE FOUND WATER, the remains of the creek that cut this ravine out of the earth, but there are dead already here. I have never seen so many. Shaking, I stumble back. The sacrificial tunic I wear is torn and darkened with dust, my feet are sore, and my throat is desert. Yet I dare not go near that water.

They stand with the creek halfway to their knees, the reek of them sickly sweet over the scent of cool water, and I want to retch. Rags hang from their shoulders. Some of them are naked, with chunks of flesh torn out of their bodies, as though my father's god tried to undo his work, ripping them apart, only to be called away, leaving his destruction unfinished.

They are lurching up out of the water; I can hear the splash of their feet. They sway like trees in wind. Their mouths gape in low moans, and the sound of them makes me weak. All their eyes are watching me. I have had men and women stare at me before, but this is different. Once a wolf watched me from a stand of terebinths and I could see the hunger in its eyes, and I ran for mother's tent, but this is different. The eyes of these dead are empty, completely empty, and they will seize me in their cold hands and drag me to their mouths and into their eyes, and I will fall into that emptiness forever.

Turning, I run, the earth hard and dry under my feet. My sides burn and I can hear myself weeping in ragged sobs.

***

They are behind me. Further back now, but I can't run like this for long, and they don't stop. I am running back uphill the way I came, and it is hard, and now there are dead ahead of me, too, three of them; they must have followed me down the defile during the night. I stumble to a stop, panting for air. The cliffs are sharp against the sky, and I want to call for my father, but I don't. I don't have the breath. Either he is there watching me and he will save me, or he won't. His stone knife waits for me, but maybe he will let these dead have me; then he won't have to cut me, and he can sleep without dreaming each night of my blood welling out over his hand. I glance behind me, so many corpses shuffling up the defile. I glance before me, the three of them getting nearer. Their hands reaching through empty air, reaching for me. I am sobbing out words of prayer to Yah and to my grandmother's gods who have no names. I don't want to be afraid; I want to face them like mother did. Even when the dead came for her, she stood and faced them, with a stick from the fire in her hand. That is the kind of woman I want to be.

***

The rock is cold in my hand, this tiny shard of the earth that one god or another shaped with his hand long before my mother or her mother or her grandmother were born. I used to take up rocks from the river by father's camp and turn them over and over in my hands for hours. Those beautiful stones, each of them a story of the place they rolled downstream from. But now I hold this one in my hand, and I can think only of its sharp edge and of how small it is, the only thing I can hold between my body and death.

The first time I swing the rock against one of the advancing corpses, my own scream startles me. My shriek does not startle the corpse; it walks right into the blow, the rock slicing through its gray skin just above its left eye. The corpse twitches and then falls to the side; my stone is stuck in its brow, and the weight of it pulls the rock from my hand. I bend and try to pull the rock out, but almost immediately I have to scramble back, because the other corpses are lurching in, their jaws opening and closing like the mouths of fish. Someone is screaming, again and again, and it might be me. Something trips me and I fall back, my hands in front of my face. One of them bends over me, its hand grasps my wrist. So cold. No life in it at all, no warmth, nothing that hears a young woman screaming and feels any pity or kinship. I am gazing through the fingers of my other hand at eyes that do not care if I live or die.

And that saves me. Because it makes me angry that they want to kill me without even caring to know my name or whether I am afraid or whether I am ready to die. It makes me furious, my blood suddenly loud in my ears. I bring one foot up and kick the ghoul hard in the face. The corpse doesn't wince or cry out or stagger back, but its head jerks to the left, and its lower jaw snaps loose. Even as I bring my knee up and slam my foot against its face again, there is a hissing in the air nearby, then another, as though small gods are flying past faster than the wind, their breath expelled in screams that are nearly silent as they rush by me. My heart has no time to wonder at it; I keep kicking wildly at the corpse's face, flesh crumpling and splitting away from my heel, its bony hand still tight around my wrist. I am screaming and screaming and finally its face breaks open and it falls back and its cold fingers fall away from my skin.

***

More of the dead lie still, some with long shafts protruding from their heads, but I haven't a moment to think about that, because several others are coming at me. I stumble to my feet, screaming my mother's name, her name, again, and again. It is all I have. I would scream a god's name, begging for his help, but what god do I really know? Yah, god of wind and fire, of hard Law written in stone, god of the phallus and the altar and the knife my father has sworn to cut me with? That god wishes to eat me, as these corpses would. My grandmother's gods, then? She was Canaanite. I wish I knew how to call to hers. I would like to pray to a god who is a woman.

***

But maybe the gods are not women and are not men either. Maybe they are like the stone of these cliffs, bleak and harsh and unforgiving, and you can't climb up to reach their blessings because the cliff face is too sheer and your fingers bleed when you try.

Or maybe the gods are dead. Everything else is.

***

It doesn't matter. What could I give to any god to make her listen to me, to make her care whether my heart keeps beating?

I can make no vow as my father did, offer nothing; I own no daughters of my own, no cattle, no tents. I am only a woman and have only my own blood and my own body. I can make no vow. I face these corpses alone, without any god, and I am screaming. My hands scrabble but find only dirt; I throw handfuls of it at the faces of the dead to blind their eyes, to make them gasp in pain and collapse to their knees; but they do not. They don't even blink. Their eyes are full of dust, and still they stumble after me. The nearest of them is terrible, naked above the waist and most of its chest hollowed out, broken ribs and emptiness inside them. One breast hangs slack above the gash. Its arm swings toward me, and I duck and dodge to the side, and then they are pressing me back against the wall of the ravine. My skin is alive with the terror of their touch, their teeth. I hold my hands before my face; in a moment I will be dead, and everything in me is cold with panic. My anger has failed me.

Their breath on my arms, dry and cold like winter night.

There is another hissing in the air near me, then another.

The corpse before me falls, toppling like a tree before the ax. Panting, I gaze about with wide eyes.

All about me, the dead are still, their heads impaled and pinned to the dry earth with javelins. A small forest of javelins has grown here while I fought.

A man is walking down the ravine toward me. The world tilts dizzily and everything blurs, but I know from his walk that he is my father.

2

MY EYES OPEN. It is dusk. Father is sitting beside me and there is firelight on his face and I can hear the cracking laughter of the small fire he has made. He is still clad in the dark, boiled leather of a raider; the last few years, I have rarely seen him in anything else. He does not take off his armor even when he stands at the altar. He wore that same armor when he stood on the high rock and made his vow to the sky, a promise, a bartering of sacrifice for victory, before lifting his javelins and springing down to do battle with the dead that were devouring us in our tents. From his belt hang two heavy gloves, so that he can handle bodies without the risk of uncleanness. A pleated skirt protects his thighs and greaves of bronze protect his legs; he took those from a caravan in return for his protection from the roaming dead. A collar of leather is fitted about his throat, as though he is a slave, but I know he wears it because he is afraid of leaving any soft place on his body open to the ghouls' teeth. My mother showed it to me once while she oiled his armor, and I saw that the inside had been worn soft as a baby's skin.

My father's armor looks no different than it did a day ago, when he sent me into the hills to meet with the god in the empty places, when he told me he would need time to pray and that I would, too. But now he has come for me.

He looks the same. Except for his hair. It is grayer than I remember it.

He has laid the stone knife across his thighs, and my breath catches when I see it. At his hip sits a bundle of javelins, bound with cord like a sheaf of barley. Their points are darkened; he hasn't wasted water to wash the dead from the wood. He has dragged the corpses into a heap, a stone's throw from our fire, to be buried beneath rocks later; to leave them uncovered would be to invite more unclean dead. I can smell them, and I shiver.

I try to sit up but find my wrists bound behind me. After struggling a moment, I bite my lip and lie still. My hands are numb. And I didn't know I could be this thirsty. The heat of it. It's as if there is a fire in my throat. There is a waterskin slung across my father's chest, and I stare at it; it is all I can do to stay still and silent. He has drunk deeply of it; the leather pouch is nearly flat against his tunic. But there is water in it, I know there is. Cool, dark water, undefiled by the feet of the dead. I want to cry.

My father feeds a little wood to the fire. Watching me without speaking. I long for him to say something, anything. Perhaps he will tell me why he has bound me or why he made the vow he did, that terrible promise, bartering his own daughter for a god's favor. Perhaps he will tell me why his face is so cold when he looks at me. Why it has always been so, even when I was small and he was tall as a mountain.

But I know why.

"Please say something, father," I whisper.

He doesn't speak.

"Please."

Still, that silence.

"Say *something*! . . . Tell me a story."

When I was small, my father could pretend I was his son, not the daughter he never wanted. He used to sit me on his knee and talk with me for hours, until the stars were out and sparks from the fire were racing up the wind like deer to meet them, and I was covering my yawns with my hand so that he would not see them and send me away to sleep. Father would talk with me about his battles or tell me a story about how he talked one of the elders in Gilead into giving him a better price on a brace of corpse-heads. Or if he'd had a little wine and his face was flushed, he'd talk about his youth in that long-ago winter when the dead first wandered into the land in vast, moaning herds. He'd tell me how Gideon led the three hundred against the unclean corpses beneath the Hill of Moreh; how Devora the prophetess brought flame and sword into all the grain fields of the land, burning out the dead, until the sky was dark with ash; how Lappidoth her husband took the tents of Shiloh and moved them into the high hills like a flock of birds alighting and settling again, veering away as at the approach of wolves. Those were the stories my father told, men's stories of fighting and battle. I mostly remember the warmth of his arm around me, and the scratch of his beard against my forehead and cheek, and the way his voice and the heat from the fire and the distant noises of the night, jackals' cries and a solitary owl, became all one murmur and glow of feeling, all one thing.

He stopped holding me like that long before my tenth

year. I began to bargain for every touch, every kind word, bringing him meals or pouring wine for him or throwing a temper in the morning before he rode out with his men. I was beaten for it a few times, and I began to hate him, but I loved him, too. I didn't understand at first why he pulled away, and I certainly didn't forgive him for it.

Now I never will.

***

"Your mother had hair dark like a river, hair like laughter at night," my father says at last. He is stirring the fire with a stick, and his eyes are full of the flames. I listen very quietly, as though I might hear between his words some way to save myself. Yet it is hard not to scream in frustration. Why is he telling me the color of her hair? I know the color of her hair.

"I was so afraid of her." The corner of his lip twitches. "I have never feared anything else as much. Until this day."

He is silent again.

Alarm at his silence grips my heart, and my irritation flickers and is gone. My mother was someone we both shared. I don't think he can kill me if he is thinking of her. That is what I hope. But I know him for a cold man who can do terrible things. He hunts the dead. He brings their scalps, swinging from his saddle, to Gilead, and brings home to us grain and beer and clothes. He and his raiders keep the dead from the fields, and in return the town keeps us supplied, and well. Mother used to wear a gown as green as well-watered leaves; I used to feel the hem between my fingertips, behind her, when she wasn't looking.

"Tell me about mother," I plead.

But he only watches the fire.

***

I don't know how much time has crawled by. He is still staring at that fire, and everywhere around us it is dark. I am afraid of him and of the unsheathed knife, which seems to burn in the firelight. And I am afraid of the dead that might see the light and come lurching toward us. Something will be done to me here, and I have no say in it. I want only to close my eyes and pretend that none of this is happening. Instead, I keep thinking of mother. How she screamed and hit at the dead with her stick. Though she raged at them, they still ate her. Nothing she did mattered. They tore her to the ground and *ate* her.

Nothing I can do matters.

There is no choice I can make, no defiance I can offer.

I am food. Either for the dead or for my father's god.

Thinking these things, I feel something dying inside me. Like leather drying and cracking in the sun.

I didn't give up at the creek. I fought. I survived until my father's javelins flitted through the air.

But whose javelins will save me now? If I struggle, twisting in these ropes, what will happen? I'll feel even more trapped; the panic that is crouching behind me in the dark will seize me, and I will scream and will never really be myself again, only a frightened animal to be laid across the altar. That is the one thing I cannot let happen. I can't die that way. I can't.

***

I have to urinate; the pressure of it inside me is hurtful. I press my thighs tightly together, struggling to think.

"Tell me about your god," I whisper. I want to understand this god who would devour me.

"He is a hungry god," my father mutters, and he tosses the charred stick onto the flaming coals. "And this is a hungry land, dead and dry. I tire of it. Our fathers should never have come here."

A tiny hope in my heart, like a moth spreading its wings in the dark. "Maybe we could leave." I wet my lips with my tongue; they are cracking. "We could go far away."

Mother suggested this to him once as they lay together on their bedding. I heard them whispering.

"I made a vow." His voice is hard.

The wings snap shut, and the moth stiffens and becomes a cold rock of anger in my heart. "What if *I* make a vow?" It is all too much, it is all too unjust. "What if I vow to your god that I will die an old woman in a tent? Or give myself to an altar in twenty years or thirty, after bearing children first to serve him?"

My father glances at me, and I see bitter amusement in his eyes.

"You are just a girl," he mutters.

My own eyes fill with tears. This is what my mother tried to tell me in all her songs: that from the day we start to breathe, what matters to us can be taken from us, is taken from us, will be taken from us, until we are bound shivering beneath a knife or until we lie choking in the dust, wrinkled and old, and the men who have been inside us or who have come out of us have left us alone, at last, in the dark. This is why she was always afraid. Yet she never shrank back.

When I lived with mother in our tent, I was a child. Now I am a woman. Not because I bled or because my breasts are swelling, but because I can look at my own death.

***

"Did you love my mother?" I whisper.

Father sits very still.

"Did you love her?" My cry is the loudest thing in the world. Louder than the fire or the dark or the distant moaning.

"As the wheat loves the dawn," he murmurs. He keeps his eyes averted.

"I am all that is left of her. Will you really watch this dry ground drink my life, or give me to flames to eat?"

His jaw tightens. "I keep my vows." He glances up, and his eyes glint in the fire. "You thirst," he says suddenly.

I try to work a little saliva in my mouth, and I nod.

He stands and unslings the waterskin from his shoulder. I can hear the voice of water splashing within it as he walks toward me. I almost cry out. Crouching, he takes my chin roughly in his hand; with his other, he opens the skin and presses the aperture to my lips. The touch of the leather is soft and warm. I suck in air desperately for a moment before I get water, cool, wonderful water, filling my mouth. I choke and splutter.

"Slowly." His voice and his hold on my chin are both rough, as though he is angry with me. But whatever fear or fury I might feel is washed away before the water like sand. Swallow after swallow. I never knew water could taste like that.

He takes it away too soon, closes the skin, and slings it back over his shoulder, rising to his feet. I make some quiet sound of pleading, some whimper or animal noise, and I am too thirsty and too tired to be ashamed of it.

As my father turns from me, he stiffens. I am staring past his ankles, and I can see that he left the knife by the coals. I think of how easily it could cut the cord about my wrists. But then my father is sweeping up a javelin from the earth, and I am watching him and not the knife, because he is striding from the fire and something hisses at him in the dark. There are eyes there, glinting with the flames. There are dead.

Several have come. They lurch into the firelight, and my father stands ready for them. He moves so fast. I have never seen anyone move so fast. It is terrifying. The edge of the javelin cuts the air like a bird's wing. He drives it through one's face; he hooks his foot behind another corpse's knee and pulls sharply, toppling it to the earth as he would any living person. It moans at him from the ground, but already he has ripped the metal point free of the first corpse and he is spinning the javelin in the air and slamming the cold, killing metal down into the head of the second. Its moan falls silent without any gasp of pain—just a silence as sudden as the darkening of a torch plunged into water.

There is a third, and it has lurched past my father and the other two. It comes right at me, its arms lifted, with a low growl. I kick wildly, pushing myself back away from the fire that is between us, even as it stumbles right into the coals. Its leg goes up in flame. For a few beats of my heart, it stands in the fire, and the flames, hungrier even than the dead, lick their way up its body, devouring, as though the dry corpse is tinder and straw. Then a sudden, gore-darkened point appears between its eyes, and its jaw goes slack. My father behind it wrenches the corpse from the fire and hurls it aside to the earth, on the point of his spear. He pulls the shaft free and stands over the burning body, his chest heaving. I glimpse my father's face in the firelight and it is terrible. As though he has seen so much death that he has almost forgotten that there is anything else to look at, anything else that he might see.

I am shaking, though I try to stop. My throat has closed tight. I cannot even scream.

My father's voice is low and hoarse. "Cairns should not wait for morning."

Piling stones above the dead, as our Hebrew ancestors have always done, crushes them to the earth, holds them in place where they can become fixed, recognizable, monumented parts of our land that nourishes us. The cairns keep the corpses from wandering, from tearing apart the tents and booths of the People. From devouring. The Ten are carved into stone tablets in far Shiloh, and stone keeps the dead in place. Stone is what our People trust the most.

My father stumbles away into the dark. He goes to gather stones for the cairns.

I lie by the fire, sobbing. I can't seem to stop. Something is broken inside me. Something is broken. My thighs go warm with my urine.

***

Mother used to sing to me while the stars came out, as they are out now. She would sit at the door of her tent and hold me, and her voice was like river and like sunset. I no longer recall what she looked like, but I remember her voice. She sings to me about sorrow and dying and falling in love and being loved and losing the one you love. When I was a little girl, I didn't understand her songs, only the beauty of her voice and the warm nearness of her. But now her words come to me, and the earth is cold under my back, the sun's heat already gone from it, and I think I understand her songs now.

I will never kiss a young man, or an old one. I will never have a man inside me. The god and I will never grow a baby together. That is what her songs are telling me. The things your heart wants are like full, ripe grapes for your thirsty throat, but they are just out of reach and maybe they will always be.

***

I lie soiled, the tunic clinging, damp, to my legs. My arms and shoulders ache with pain. Yet I am hardly aware of that. Quiet has come to my heart after the tears, and I am thinking. When my father returns from raising the cairns, my eyes are dry. Part of me wants to struggle again, but I don't. I lift my head a little, one side of my face covered in dust. I wish I could wash it from my skin.

He crouches by the coals and sets his fingertips on the stone blade. He doesn't look at me; if he is aware that I have wet myself, he shows no sign of it. I stare at the flames, thinking for the first time not of the knife but of what will come after: my father will lay me across dry tinder, and once I have bled, my body will be burned, and wherever his god lives in the sky, he will breathe in the smoke and the scent of me, and be fed. Strangely, I feel no dread now, only a deep quiet. The dance of the few small flames among the coals fascinates me; I can't look away from it. Though my body hurts as though I've been beaten, there is a fullness in my breast, and I realize that this moment by this fire, and even my father's silence, is a gift. My mother died with so many words still on her lips—things she might have said to me, or to her god, or to my father. Things she never had the chance to say. But I have that chance. I can say the things that need to be said. Because he is not speaking, and he is not lifting the knife. And because I am a woman, not a child. Because he is giving me this last gift, this moment to speak. He might command me to silence, but I might not obey him. He might beat me until I do. But he is not doing any of these things. Maybe he is thinking of mother, too. Maybe he is remembering that she never said farewell to him. I don't know. But I am grateful for this moment.

I work a little spit in my mouth and speak.

"You wanted a son." Despite my efforts, my voice is little more than a hoarse whisper.

His eyes moisten, and seeing that, my voice breaks.

"I hope you find another wife," I tell him, "and that she gives you one."

I don't know why I must die. He brought me water and watched over me, and kept the dead away. Yet he can't be dissuaded, because he always does—has always done—what he feels he has to do.

"I love you, father."

It is the first time in years that I have said those words.

I can't be sure, but I think they are true.

I don't know why they should be true. It has been long since he has held me or even spoken my name; he does not say it or acknowledge it now. But his eyes are no longer cold. And he is my father. And whether the words I say are true or not, or only partly true, I need to say them. Otherwise I will have wasted the gift of this moment. They are the right words to say. It is a way of saying farewell.

I glance once at his face, then at the flames. Shivering, I close my eyes.

"I am ready to die," I whisper.

***

A wind rustles the grasses on the cliffs above us. After a while, I hear him get up. Then a furtive step. And another.

I keep my eyes closed for a long time.

My body goes hot with anger. How can he do this to me? I have said my farewell. Maybe his only farewell will be the slide of that knife across my throat. But he is not giving me even that. He is prolonging this, and it is cruel. I regret telling him that I love him. He is cold and cruel, and his god is cold and cruel, as well.

"Father?"

There is no answer.

Opening my eyes, I find I am alone and surrounded by the cairns of the silent dead.

He is gone.

I lie there, bound, just breathing. Fighting down panic. Did he step away a moment for prayer, or is he really leaving me here? Bound, like this? To starve or be eaten? Maybe he has struck some new and perverse bargain with his god—he will sacrifice me, but not by his own hand. Instead he will leave me for the wandering dead—bound, helpless, powerless to choose the moment of my own death.

I draw in another shuddering breath. That is what I wanted, I realize. To choose the moment that I would die. That's why I fought the corpses, why I gave father my farewell, why I told him when I was ready. And now he has taken even this from me.

I scream, making the cliffs echo with my cry.

But only once.

3

THE ROCKS HERE ARE BROKEN and sharp-edged, as though Yah has been pounding on the hill with his foot, year after year, trying to shatter it. My father has not come back, and the fire he made is only coals. The stars are also coals, without warmth. I am shivering. I can't tell whether the sounds on the slope above are wind or the moaning dead.

My death is my own to make.

This thought is clear and cold in my mind, like ice on water.

Sawing the ropes against a jagged stone makes my hands sting with pain, and my blood is warm and sticky where it flows down over my fingers. It takes a long time, but finally the ropes snap free, and I bring my hands in front of me, clutching one wrist numbly with the other. My hands hurt with returning life, so that I have to bite my sleeve to keep from screaming. My breath comes ragged.

If the dead are what I hear moaning on the hill, they are loud and close. My father has forgotten me. He is gone. I would be numb with the pain of it, but my heart is thunder inside me, and my fear is ripping at me the way summer hail tears holes through green leaves.

I don't want to die. So I must be stronger than my fear, faster than my terror.

Though my hands still hurt, I walk quickly to one of the cairns, where my father has leaned a javelin against the stones. I can see that the bronze point is broken, as though chipped against a bone, but it still looks sharp. My father should not have left it. There are others, several, with the points thrust into the dirt between the cairns so that they stand like thin, leafless trees. Briefly I wonder if my father *meant* to leave them for me, like this, or if he left these here for some other purpose known only to his own heart or to his god. The wooden shafts are slender, and I can carry two in my right hand and leave my left hand free. I don't know how to throw them as my father did, so that they strike where I wish, but I can stab with them. That is what I will do.

***

They are coming. There are four of them, moving downhill toward the water behind me. I can't see them, but I can hear the shuffling of their feet. I can smell them. I wait in a crouch with the javelins, and I can hear my own blood. The night is sharp. I hold my death close; it is my own, and these unsteady corpses will not take it from me.

They are nearer.

I try to count, to calm my heartbeat, but it doesn't work; the rising numbers make me anxious. So I start to recite the names of the god silently, without moving my lips. Though I don't know which names I can trust, or whether all these names belong to a god who wants me dead, they are all beautiful.

Yah.

Elohim.

El Shaddai.

El Olam.

Yah Yireh.

Yah Nissi.

Adonai.

These are the names of the god, but I don't know if that god is harsh like my father or kind like my mother. Though my mother called out the same names my father did, she sang about a god who is a giver of life, a god of the womb. That kind of god would give me breath, hold me while I weep, then pull me to my feet and tell me to stand as my mother did. A stick in my hand.

The shambling footsteps are near, and I can see the dead silhouetted against the dark and the faint, faint glint of their eyes. I leap to my feet and plunge one of the javelins up and forward with a shout. My arm is strong and fast, and there is little resistance as the javelin spears through a corpse's face in the dark. Even as the other closes with me, the first falls to the side. Wood cracks like a bone breaking, and I am holding in my right hand only a splintered haft, while the rest remains in the corpse at my feet; I cast aside the haft with a cry. Now I hold only one. These are my father's tools; of course they would be of two minds about protecting me.

Cold fingers grasp my shoulder. I lunge aside, and the corpse comes with me; my heartbeat is wild. I thrust the length of the javelin crosswise between me and the corpse's throat. The thing's teeth snap in the air, so near my face. That winter, winter breath. Tears on my face. I cry when I am scared. But then, I have seen even my father do that, once. Frantically, under my breath I gasp the names, and the recitation is all that holds me together, a wall of words raised like hard stones against the wind of panic. El Olam. Yah Nissi. Yah Yireh. Yah Yireh, Yah Yireh. I can't find any other names, any other words, everything is gone from my mind; there is only the clack of those teeth, a finger's width from my skin, and the burn in my arm as I fight against its weight, fight to hold it at bay with that slender length of terebinth wood. I recite that last name over and over: Yah Yireh, Yah Yireh.

Then we are on the earth. I must have stumbled. Shoving my knee into the corpse's belly, I throw my weight to the side and roll up onto it, and then my fingers are in its eyes. I have let go of the javelin; I am just digging my hands into its face, as though I am kneading dough with my mother. And I keep doing it, my heart pounding, pounding. And then it is still.

So still.

I have survived again.

I glide along the knife's edge of my fear, the exhilaration of being alive, *still* alive, lifting me the way the god's unseen hands lift a bird into the sky. The small sound of my tears hitting the dead flesh beneath me. The rasping of my breath in my throat. Taking up the javelin quickly, I get to my feet. Still panting, Yah, Yah, Yah. Yes, yes. Yes. I live. Yes. Yes.

I am panting, here in the empty night. I don't know if there are other dead nearby. The air is still. At the warmth

trickling over my wrist, I glance down. I can't see, but suddenly I feel my nails biting into my palm, where I hold the one javelin I retain deathly tight. With a low moan, I open my hand. The pain is sharp, but it is also good, because I am alive. Drawing in quick, shuddering breaths, I step around the corpses. I should cover them with stones, as my father would, but I fear staying here. I will leave them behind, the way we leave all our dead behind in the end. I will walk out alone into the dark, not knowing what my feet will find, or what will find me.

4

I REEK, AND I HATE IT. I found a tuft of wild grass in the dry dust, tore it up and scrubbed my legs until I bled a little, but though I am drier, I smell like urine and the dead. The smell is in the white tunic; it is even in my hair. I would cut away my hair if I could. I want to smell like me again.

Though my hands shake with fear, I am walking uphill now. Not toward the creek behind. The dead are by that stream; I know that now. If I want to escape them, if I want to live, I must climb up these hills, up toward the roof of the world. There is water there, too; rain falls and collects in small pools in the rock on the high slopes, and if I walk north, toward White Cedars, if I go far north, there will be trees, and maybe I can find honey to eat. That will be dangerous, too, because I will have to break into it with a stick or with my hands, and the bees will hurt me when I run, with honeycomb in my hands, to flee them. I will have to find some place to hide from the bees before I attempt it. Maybe I can find cool mud, or . . . maybe there will be food other than honey. Berries, if any grow that high, or bird's eggs, or maybe I could catch a small animal. That would be better than honey, and safer than bees.

But I don't know what to expect. I have never been in these hills.

I whisper old stories to myself as I walk, every story my father told about ancestors of ours who fought in the Ramat ha-Golan. I am searching for anything that could help me. Anything that was said about the places to the north, the places uphill.

Because I am going to live, to the last moment I can.

My mother died, and she might live only in me. Who else will remember her name?

Who will remember mine?

My father might have other children, but they will be with other wives, women I don't know. My name is mine alone to carry. I may die of cold once I am up higher, or worse, I may die of thirst and the terrible drying of my body—but I will *not* be eaten. I am walking uphill, toward the sky where my father's god lives. And if, when I get up there, where there is nothing but empty air between me and the stars, if I hear his god calling, I will call back, and I will demand that he answer me. That he tell me why he wants me to die.

If I die, I will choose the moment of it.

I do not want to die.

**

I have tried a few times now to climb out of this ravine, but in some places the rock is sheer, and in others it crumbles under my weight. I am frustrated, and it is so hard to keep the panic from my mind. Every time I hear a moan behind me, back toward the water, every time some small desert mouse skitters among the loose pebbles beneath some dried bush ahead of me, I startle like a rabbit and nearly bolt. I cannot do that. I cannot. My mother would not startle like that. I have to just breathe slowly and walk, keep walking, and not stop, not ever.

There must be a way out of this ravine.

There must.

***

Has my father left the ravine? Is he somewhere ahead of me or somewhere behind? That uncertainty is what makes me jump at each sound, more than the thought of the dead and their teeth. He took his knife with him; men don't leave their knives out for the weather. He might come back. He might still lay me bound across an altar of warm rock and cut me open. My eyes moisten, but I blink back the tears furiously. I must not think of my father. He left me bound in the night by the cairns, as though I were dead already, awaiting my turn for burial. If he had meant to go through with sacrificing me, surely he would have made his altar and then waited by me for the dawn, to fulfill his vow. I asked him to. I told him I was ready. And he walked away. He is not coming back.

***

Wind has come up, and the noises it makes in the rocks are frightening. Worse, it has torn clouds out of some secret place in the sky, and they have taken away the stars. It is so dark, I can't see the ground. It's not always easy to tell where the moaning comes from. It has to be behind me. I hope it is behind me.

Mother told me once about the winter when she was younger than I and she got lost in a wood. She told me how her heart threw itself against her breast like a wild thing, but she also told me how she sang softly, under her breath, and how the song warmed her and calmed her until she found the edge of the wood and saw the smoke of her father's camp and ran, laughing, from the trees toward its fires. But I don't dare sing. Something that doesn't live might hear me.

***

I have found it. I knew there had to be a way out. And there is. I might have missed it in the dark, but the ravine has narrowed, and I have started running my fingers along the near wall and running the haft of the javelin quietly along the far wall as I walk.

And here it is: a narrow dip in the rock, and a few steps up it becomes almost a tunnel, with just a tiny gap of air above my head. Some of the rock is worn smooth; water must come down here, singing and splashing, in wetter months. Now it is dry, but the footholds are still difficult. I have to use one hand to help bear my weight and steady me as I move carefully upward. At one point I have to press the javelin into the crook of my shoulder and hold it there, awkwardly, with my head tilted to the side, so that I can use both my hands. The ascent becomes steeper, and I press my belly to the rock. After days of dry earth, this smooth rock is unsettling; it is as though I am squirming my way up the gullet of some giant animal. Vertigo makes me clench my eyes shut. I cling to the rock, breathing hard, until I can convince myself that I am not falling upward.

Then I climb. My breathing is too loud between these walls of stone.

But then the rock around me opens up, and there is sky again. Even as I step out of the ravine, the clouds part above me—at last!—and there is starlight. I stand and breathe, feeling the cold air fill my body. Though I am exhausted, I have never felt so awake. I am like a deer, alert to every sound, every scent in the air. I listen. I watch. I am silhouetted against the stars, but nothing moans or lurches toward me.

There are dry grasses beneath my feet, and as the wind picks up, it hisses in the blades. I gaze down at them, then at my feet, which I see are cracked and bleeding. I came barefoot to this high land, a sacrifice for a god whose hunger is wide as the sky. But it is the rocks and now the grasses that have been drinking from me. I feel no faintness at the sight of my blood or the bruises on my feet and ankles. I have seen so much this day, I do not think I will ever feel faint at anything again.

Glancing up, I find the star that mother called North. And that tells me that I am on the wrong side of the ravine, the southern side. Only a few trees are up here, lonely things, but I can see where there are more, across the ravine and in the distance, where there must be water. I might be able to leap across here; the walls of the ravine are close together, but it is a frightening gap at my feet, and in the dark beneath is cold death and thirst and the lurching corpses. I must find some place where it is narrower.

I begin to run, ignoring the soreness of my feet. I run along the edge of the defile, using the starlight. This ravine cannot be forever; there will be a better way across.

***

In this desolation, far from my father's tents and my father's stories, I think that maybe the god *is* a woman, beset as I am by the dark and by the day's heat. I do not know my father's god, whose meal I would have been. I think my mother's god is running beside me in the dark, like a deer, and we flee the hunger of the earth together, and it is men, living or dead, who would devour us.

5

By THE STARLIGHT I see that the two corpses ahead of me are desiccated. Dried up, like bodies left in the desert. Even the stench is gone. The eyes, too, eaten by birds. I approach and crouch near them, with my javelin held across my thighs. I don't feel sick looking at these, only sad. These were people. They were a man and a woman; I only know this because the man's phallus lies crooked and dry across his hip, a flaccid, withered length like the husk shed by a serpent. I saw the men dancing, drunk, at the fire once, outside the tents. They were stiff and frightening. But this man is dead, and his spear is only a limp stretch of skin, after all.

The other has the wide hips of a mother. Were these two man and wife, or man and slave, or brother and sister fleeing, as I am fleeing? Like me, lost in the dark? If they were walking toward the heights, as I am, they never made it there. I still can.

I suck in a breath and rise to my feet, but suddenly one of the corpses stirs, the dry sound of its hand scraping across the grit. I nearly drop the javelin, stumbling back so quickly.

The corpse crawls on its hands toward me, dragging its legs behind it. With a cry I jab my javelin at its head, but it grasps the wood just above the bronze point and wrenches the weapon forward, and me with it; I scream as I lose my footing and fall to my knees. The thing grips my arm and pulls me down and it is on top of me, so strong. Its long teeth snap by my ear. Its breath is so *cold*, its burn on my skin like the first touch of frostbite. I am screaming and screaming, and kicking. Panic has eaten my mind. I slam my arm against its throat, trying to push it up and off me. Its hand grips my face. I scrabble at the rocks and dust, trying to find my javelin, but I can't, it isn't there. I can't see, I can't breathe, my heart is loud and this is it, I am going to die.

But I have squirmed aside just a little, and I have my hip beneath it and I lunge, and we are rolling. Its cold fingers catch at my tunic, but my struggle and my climb among the rocks has torn the cloth, and I tear loose, leaving my garment behind in the corpse's grip. I scramble away on my hands and knees, with the hiss of its breath behind me. My hand strikes the javelin, and I grasp it, then leap to my feet and run and *run*. The air is cold on my body, but I don't feel it. My blood is rushing everywhere inside me, and there is only the slap of the dry earth against my feet and the snarling thing pursuing me. Then the ravine opens beneath me, and I hurl my javelin across the gap, hear it clatter against the rocks even as I spring, leaping across the empty dark with a shriek.

The ground strikes my belly, and my legs kick at empty air. I clutch at loose soil. Falling. But my foot finds a root, a root! I put my weight on it and thrust myself upward, even as I hear the wood creak as though about to break, and I throw my breast up onto the cliff. My left hand finds a tussock of weeds, and I pull myself up, groaning, my lungs burning. I get my legs up and roll onto my back, and I am sobbing, shaking. The night above me has been shot through with stars, as though warriors have hurled spears through the tent of night and left those shining holes behind. I clutch the earth with my fingers, afraid I might fall off into that dark cloth of sky. I can hear the corpse shambling along the far edge of the ravine, and I can hear its shuddering moan. I shut my eyes tightly and just breathe, just breathe.

I have lost my breath, my tunic, everything but the javelin nearby. I am naked in the dark. But I am alive.

Fierce joy in my heart. I am alive.

Men, living and dead, are often stronger than we. But not always smarter, or faster.

I am alive. And undevoured.

The corpse on the far brink moans again, and that long, lonely wail fills the night. My eyes open again on the stars.

I will not fear that moan.

Let men, living or dead, moan as they will. They cannot ever truly have us, truly devour us. My death remains my own to choose.

Great gulps of air. I fill my body with air.

Maybe if I can just breathe in enough, I will lift from the earth like a bird. All those stars—I would like to fly through them into whatever bright world lies outside this tent in which we and the god are trapped. Maybe outside, there is no hunger.

My face is still wet from my tears when I stand and look about. The land before me is wide, and I walk out into it, moving quickly, leaving the cry of that corpse and all my dead behind.

6

I HAVE REACHED the roof of the world. No one told me it would be this beautiful. The trees here are stunted but dark with needles, and the wind blows my hair back, stings my eyes, and raises goosebumps on my arms and breasts. I wear no white for sacrifice; no man has clothed me for his purpose or his god's; I stand naked and my own. I smell water. And the stars, and the stars.

There are no dead here, and this javelin I carry is only dead wood that I have brought with me out of a memory. This wind has carried away my death. With a single breath, a sigh as I gazed out at these dark plateaus, my death leapt from me into the air. I throw my head back and shout my name, and give it to the wind, too. Let that wind take it, too, far away, where no one will remember it. They will think me dead at my father's bloody hands. Let them. My father took that life from me, but he also set me free into these hills. I still breathe. I still walk on this wind, between earth and sky. If my father's god or my mother's is up here among these stars, let that god fly with me. If not, I will fly alone. This is not one of my father's stories, not a story of my tribe. I do not know what this story will be, but I am the one telling it. That girl who had a name and a tribe, a mother and a father, and a tent in which to sleep, she is slain and dead.

Only I remain.

JUDGES 11:40

FOR GENERATIONS after the dead were cleansed from those hills, the young women of that tribe would walk up into the dry and thirsty places after the coming of their first blood, in memory of Yeptha's daughter. Though they could not remember her name, the young women used her story to understand their own predicament, the predicament of being young women.

They wandered the ravines for four days and four nights, neither bathing nor changing their clothes. Before returning to the tents, each woman would face the inevitable truth of her own death and learn to hold it close. Each would weep for Yeptha's daughter; she would weep for the changes in her own body and for the suffering she knew she would face as a woman in a land where either the dead or the living might devour her. She and all her sisters would weep until the land echoed with their cries, and their cries were such that neither the world, nor men, nor mighty Yah could find any silence in which to hide from their voices.

ACKNOWLEDGMENTS

I DO NOT stand alone.

Andrew Hallam read this manuscript for me; Juliet Ulman edited it with compassion and insight. My readers and Patreon members gave me fierce encouragement. My wife Jessica and my daughters River and Inara teach me each day about the strength of women.

I am grateful to all of you.

This story is for you.

***

WITH SPECIAL THANKS TO

THEA DEE, RON GIESECKE, ANDREA G MANN, DARREN WAGNER, JEREMY KERR, SCOTT ROCHAT, JUHI MENDIRATTA, KATY FLYNN, TODD BERGMAN, AND ALL MY PATREON MEMBERS WHO HAVE HELPED FUND THIS SILVER EDITION!

ABOUT THE AUTHOR

STANT LITORE doesn't consider his writing a vocation; he considers it an act of survival. As a youth, he witnessed the 1992 outbreak in the rural Pacific Northwest firsthand, as he glanced up from the feeding bins one dawn to see four dead staggering toward him across the pasture, dark shapes in the morning fog. With little time to think or react, he took a machete from the barn wall and hurried to defend his father's livestock; the experience left him shaken. After that, community was never an easy thing for him. The country people he grew up with looked askance at his later choice of college degree and his eventual graduate research on the history of humanity's encounters with the undead, and the citizens of his college community were sometimes uneasy at the machete and rosary he carried with him at all times, and at his grim look. He did not laugh much, though on those occasions when he did the laughter came from him in wild guffaws that seemed likely to break him apart. As he became book-learned, to his own surprise he found an intense love of ancient languages, a fierce admiration for his ancestors, and a deepening religious bent. On weekends, he went rock-climbing in the cliffs without rope or harness, his fingers clinging to the mountain, in a furious need to accustom himself to the nearness of death and teach his body to meet it. A rainstorm took him once on the cliffs and he slid thirty-five feet and hit a ledge without breaking a single bone, and concluded that he was either blessed or reserved in particular for a fate far worse. He married a girl his parents considered a heathen woman, but whose eyes made him smile. She persuaded him to come down from the cliffs, and he persuaded her to wear a small covenant ring on her hand, spending what coin he had to make it one that would shine in starlight and whisper to her heart how much he prized her. Desiring to live in a place with fewer trees (though he misses the forested slopes of his youth), a place where you can scan the horizon for miles and see what is coming for you while it is still well away, he settled in Colorado with his wife and two daughters, and they live there now. The mountains nearby call to him with promises of refuge. Driven again and again to history with an intensity that burns his mind, he corresponds in his thick script for several hours each evening with scholars and archaeologists and even a few national leaders or thugs wearing national leaders' clothes who hoard bits of forgotten past in far countries. He tells stories of his spiritual ancestors to any who will come by to listen, and he labors to set those stories to paper. Sometimes he lies awake beside his sleeping wife and listens in the night for any moan in the hills, but there is only her breathing, soft and full, and a mystery of beauty beside him. He keeps his machete sharp but hopes not to use it.

zombiebible@gmail.com
@thezombiebible
www.stantlitore.com
www.facebook.com/stant.litore

DID YOU ENJOY
THE STORY?

IF YES, consider joining my Patreon membership:
http://www.patreon.com/stantlitore

I use Patreon to fund my independent work and to make it possible for my fiction to support the needs of my disabled, three-year-old daughter Inara. You can learn more at my Patreon page—and if you join as one of my members there, I will send you ebooks!

You can also reach me at zombiebible@gmail.com. I look forward to hearing what you thought of the story!

STANT LITORE
FEBRUARY 2016